For Tara, who aims bravely for the skies — P B
For Adam — C J

HODDER CHILDREN'S BOOKS
First published in Great Britain in 2021 by Hodder and Stoughton

1 3 5 7 9 10 8 6 4 2

Text and illustrations copyright © Hachette Children's Group, 2021
Written by Peter Bently • Illustrated by Chris Jevons

HB ISBN 978 1 444 95410 4 • PB ISBN 978 1 444 95411 1

Printed and bound in China

Hodder Children's Books
An imprint of Hachette Children's Group
Part of Hodder and Stoughton
Carmelite House, 50 Victoria Embankment, London, EC4Y 0DZ

An Hachette UK Company
www.hachette.co.uk
www.hachettechildrens.co.uk

Hodder
Children's
Books

Peter Bently & Chris Jevons

Snow White IN SPACE

Up in her space station, Captain Snow White
Saw a strange ship zooming past in the night.
"It's an alien spaceship! Who can it be?
I'll take a quick trip in my shuttle to see!"

She reached the
strange spaceship,
and saw . . .

A PROUD QUEEN,
Who spoke to a glimmering,
shimmering screen:
"Robot, robot on the wall,
who is the SMARTEST of them all?

No need to say. It's **ME**, I know —
Mortilda, Queen of Planet Zo!
With my robot army soon I'll be
the ruler of this galaxy!"

The robot said,
"You're smart, it's true.
But **SNOW WHITE**
is smarter still than you.
And you'd better watch out.
She's just outside . . ."

"AFTER HER!"
Mortilda cried.

"Yikes!" said Snow White, as she fled into space
With the queen close behind in a furious chase . . .

On Pluto, Snow White saw a cave, dark and wide.
"Fantastic," she said. "What a good place to hide!"

But Mortilda had seen her and cackled with glee,
"Let's get her, robotlings! Quick, follow me!"

The queen and her robots
ran after Snow White
Through long, twisting
tunnels as black as the night.

"Where am I going?
I really can't tell.
And surely that can't be
CHOCOLATE I smell?"

She tripped and cried out,
"Now they'll catch me,
for sure!"

Then she spotted a very
small door near the floor.
She wriggled inside it and
shut the door fast . . .

. . . Just as Mortilda went hurtling past!

She stood very still, as quiet as a mouse.

Then a scared little voice said,

"Who's **THIS** in our house?"

"Oh!" said Snow White as she spun round to see . . .

... Seven small aliens having their tea!

"Hello!" she said kindly. "My name is Snow White.
I'm terribly sorry I gave you a fright."

"Don't worry, young Earthling," an alien said.
"Would you like a hot muffin with chocolate spread?
Our names are Puggle and Fuggle and Blee,
Nik, Nak and Noo-Nah. And Stanley — that's me!"

Blee said, "We work at the chocolate lake.
Do you fancy a slice of our double-choc cake?"

Snow White said, "Sorry, I really must go.
I have to defeat Queen Mortilda of Zo!"
She told them what happened and how she had fled.
"Please let us help you!" the aliens said.

"But how can we beat all those robots?" said Stan. "Well," Snow White chuckled, "I've just had a plan . . ."

Out in the tunnel as dark as the night,
The queen cried out crossly,
"WHERE ARE YOU, SNOW WHITE?
My robots will capture you soon, do you hear?"
Then Snow White popped up and said,
"Hey! Over here!"

With the robots behind her,
she ran down a slope . . .

. . . To where Fuggle and Stanley
were holding a rope.

"Now!" said Snow White
as she swung off the ledge —
And the robots went tumbling
over the edge!

"No!" shrieked the queen.
But the bots couldn't stop —
And they fell in the chocolate
lake with a **PLOP!**

And then the queen saw, on the cavern's great wall,

The shape of a monster, enormous and tall.

Closer and closer the space monster loomed.

"I hear intruders. I'll **EAT** them!" it boomed.

"ARGH!" yelled Mortilda
and, quick as a flash,
She fled to her ship in a
scrambling dash.

"I'm going home!"
wailed the terrified queen.
Then she zoomed back to Zo
and was never more seen.

"OK, it's safe now. She's gone!" grinned Snow White.
As the chocolate-cake monster came into the light.

Stan said, "Your plan was a smart one, all right!"
"I couldn't have done it alone," smiled Snow White.
"Thank you, my friends. Now I'd better head back —

As soon as I've had a nice
CHOCOLATE CAKE snack!"